Charlie Dragon

Charlie Dragon

Molly Bond

Illustrated by the author

HODDER AND STOUGHTON
LONDON SYDNEY AUCKLAND TORONTO

For Dan and Jo

British Library Cataloguing in Publication Data
Bond, Molly
  Charlie Dragon. – (Brock blue)
  I. Title   II. Series
  823'.914[J]   PZ7

  ISBN 0-340-39241-X

First published 1986

Published by Hodder and Stoughton Children's Books,
a division of Hodder and Stoughton Ltd,
Mill Road, Dunton Green, Sevenoaks, Kent TN13 2YJ

Photoset by Rowland Phototypesetting Ltd,
Bury St Edmunds, Suffolk

Printed in Great Britain by T. J. Press (Padstow) Ltd,
Padstow, Cornwall

Chapter 1

George, clutching Mum's old brown coat, was trying to keep up with her as she battled her way down the wet street with push-chair and carrier bags, the rain dribbling down his neck from her umbrella. His year-old sister Rosie sat hunched up and scowling in the buggy, a cabbage on her lap.

George had a worry, but for the moment he had forgotten it, for that Saturday afternoon they were on their way to the Fairy Grotto – 'Special Christmas Attraction'. They weren't real fairies of course, although Rosie was still young enough to think they were. It wasn't a proper grotto either: it was behind a faded red curtain, off the Carpet and Bedding Department of Boddis & Geerings, the largest shop in town.

'Follow the Footprints to Fairyland' announced a notice as they pushed through the swing doors into a gush of hot scented air.

'Hold on to that cabbage,' Mum said to Rosie as they followed the black footprints, like Man Friday's in *Robinson Crusoe*, winding between the counters of gloves and dangling beads, and shiny handbags stacked on racks. George placed his feet carefully on each large footprint.

'Don't drag, George,' shouted Mum over her shoulder as, engulfed by shoppers, she disappeared with Rosie down the wide staircase to the basement where the black footprints led.

'Keep up, do,' she said, 'or you'll be swallowed up in this crush.'

At the bottom of the stairs were counters with rolls of dress materials. It was then that George remembered his worry. It was in his trouser pocket, where he'd stuffed it back after showing Mum: a crumpled piece of paper from his teacher, Mrs Trimble, that read:

Dear Parents,

We are holding our annual Fancy Dress Party on the afternoon of Friday 15th December, and as in previous years your co-operation in providing your child with a costume, preferably home-made, would be very much appreciated. There will be a prize for the most original.

Yours sincerely,
Deirdre Trimble

It gave George an awful sinking feeling just being there in his pocket. Friday 15th December! Only two weeks away! For George it was the very worst day in the whole year. All the other children in the class had costumes to make you gasp. Their parents spent hours transforming them into Supermen or Goldilocks, dinosaurs or Oxo cubes. George's best friend

Tom Toogood was going as a robot. His Dad had his own workshop behind their house. It was full of whining saws and sanders, power lathes and whirring drills. He made shelves and cupboards and kitchen units, and when Tom's Mum said she'd really more than enough, he made Tom a tree-house for the summer and a toboggan for the snow. And for Fancy Dress Parties he made him amazing and ingenious outfits, transforming Tom into an astronaut last year and Spider Man the year before. Mr Toogood was probably in the Do-It-Yourself Shop now, buying up the robot parts, and every evening from now until the Party he would be in his workshop sawing and sanding, welding and spraying until Tom had a costume that would be the envy of all.

It was no good George asking Dad to turn him into a Superman, or even a box of cornflakes. Dad could barely bang in a nail. It took him half a year to make a bookshelf, and when it was up it was so crooked the books slid off.

And Mum couldn't sew. She could only 'cojjel', which was her word for bunching up a wodge of material, stuffing it against another piece of material, and jabbing at them with a needle threaded with cotton that didn't match. Last year when George had handed her the dreaded piece of paper she had given up altogether. She had ripped up an old sheet, cut out two frayed holes for eyes with blunt scissors, smudged on a black blob with a felt pen for a nose, and another for a mouth, had put the whole thing

over George's head, and told him he was a snowman.

'The simplest costumes are the best,' she had said with satisfaction, winding one of Dad's old scarves round his neck as a finishing touch. 'You'll see.'

But George hadn't been able to see at all. For no sooner had the Party started, with them all parading round the playground in a big circle, than Tom, who had been behind him, had stepped on a piece of the sheet that was dragging on the ground behind George. Immediately the 'eyes' had shot up over his head, and with no holes to look through, all George had been able to see was thick white fog. He had groped around for a while in the folds of sheet, until

8

he realised that the sounds of the chattering class had died away. He had found an opening in the sheet at last and had peered out to find he was standing alone in an empty playground. While he had been fumbling around in the fog the rest of the class had filed back into the hall. Mrs Trimble had sent Tom, in his dazzling astronaut costume, to fetch George and bring him back into the hall. Not only had no-one had the least idea what George was supposed to be, but because he couldn't see through the thick white fog, and kept losing his arms and falling over his feet, Mrs Trimble had had to grasp him by the shoulders to steer him round the hall.

His worry was that this year Mum had said he could wear the same old piece of sheet and go as a ghost.

He had been reminded of his worry by seeing Fenella Throgmorton's mother buying up lengths of shiny red velvet. Last year it had been lengths of frilly nylon net. Mrs Throgmorton always got her ideas from Boddis & Geerings' Fairy Grotto. Last year Fenella went as Cinderella – Cinderella after her Fairy Godmother had waved her wand over her, not in her rags of course. Everyone had gasped in admiration and said 'What a beautiful costume!' and the teachers had said how clever Mrs Throgmorton was with her needle, and Fenella had won the prize. George hadn't been able to see her through the fog, but he had heard them all exclaiming.

The queue to the Fairy Grotto was very long. It

started by the rows of beds, wound round the piles of rush mats stacked like pancakes, on between rolls of rose-splodged carpet to the faded red curtain with a notice above it which said: 'Fairy Grotto – Adults 30p, children 20p'.

'It's daylight robbery,' Mum said, fumbling in her carrier bag for her purse. 'They put the price up every year.'

You shouldn't have to pay to see fairies, George thought crossly, especially as they aren't real. Seeing Mrs Throgmorton had depressed him, his socks were still soggy from the rain and the queue was moving so slowly. Rain-water was trickling off Mum's folded umbrella and forming little puddles on the floor.

Chapter 2

It was dark in the Grotto. They shuffled down a tunnel until they came to what was supposed to be a cave. It was lit by eerie green and blue lights, and although George knew the cave wasn't real, it was just a bit scary. Three gnomes with fixed smiles were sitting round a pond, fishing. Their heads were nodding slowly up and down and the hands that weren't holding the fishing lines were moving slowly from side to side. They looked stupid and scary at the same time. Rosie's eyes were huge and staring from beneath her plastic hood.

George looked round to make sure Mum was still there. In her wellingtons and old brown coat, with her woollen scarf tied over her head, she kept disappearing into the gloom. Mum was short and round with a comforting lap for climbing into when he needed a cuddle, but sometimes he wished she looked like Mrs Throgmorton, tall and smart in her bright red coat with its froths of fur round the collar, with her shiny gold hair, and her high-heeled shoes with glittery blobs on the toe. The only blobs Mum ever had on her shoes were blobs of grease from the chip pan.

'Seen enough?' asked Mum, wiping Rosie's nose

and stuffing back the cabbage that was nearly rolling out of the push-chair.

'Let's see what's round the corner.'

In the next cave the lights that shone out of the make-believe rocks were red and orange. They lit up a brass bedstead with a patchwork quilt. George remembered seeing one like it in the Furniture Department just before they came into the Grotto, with a card on it which said £350. It had seemed an awful lot of money to pay for something as boring as a bed. Now here it was again but with a wolf wearing gold-rimmed spectacles and a frilly nightcap, propped up against the pillows. The wolf kept opening and closing its mouth, showing a lot of teeth. By the bed stood Red Riding Hood with her basket of eggs. Her arm, too, was moving stiffly from side to side, as if she couldn't decide what to do with the eggs. Fenella Throgmorton, thought George gloomily. He imagined her at the Fancy Dress Party, in her shiny red cloak, being handed the prize, a pleased-with-herself smile on her face, and everyone clapping. And he imagined himself, draped in last year's sheet, with the 'face' sliding up over his head. The sinking feeling came back.

Rosie's eyes were fixed on the wolf's teeth and her mouth was turning down at the corners. Mum hustled her out before she started screaming, George holding on to the hem of her coat just to make sure she didn't disappear.

'Let's hope the scene in the last cave is a bit more

cheerful,' said Mum over her shoulder. 'I could do with a good laugh.'

But a white and lifeless Sleeping Beauty, lying on yet another bed from the Furniture Department, was even more dismal. The cardboard walls were painted grey to look like those of a castle. Through a hole in the cardboard they could see the Prince in a golden crown, with eyes that opened and shut very slowly. They reminded George of Dad's eyes, trying to keep awake in front of the telly. On the other side of the cardboard wall there were rubber snakes and plastic toads between large white pebbles, and stuck to the wall were three plastic lizards. Mum didn't mind toads and frogs and lizards out of doors where they belonged, but in here, with the eerie mauve lights shining on them, they gave her the creeps.

'Urgh,' she shuddered, and Rosie started to howl.

'She's had enough,' said Mum thankfully. 'Come on, my feet are killing me. Let's get a breath of fresh air. I can't wait to get home and have a nice cup of tea.' And she vanished round a cardboard rock with the screaming Rosie.

But George had noticed something rather odd about the smallest lizard. Unlike the other two which were green, its scales were sparkling and all colours of the rainbow. The little bumps that ran along its back were gold, and its claws a glistening silver. Its eyes shone like rubies. But the strangest thing was the puffs of smoke coming out of its nostrils.

That's clever, thought George; more ingenious

than Red Riding Hood's stupid arm going from side to side all day long, day after day, week after week; or the Prince's eyes opening and shutting as though he were about to drop off to sleep. The puffs of smoke made the lizard look almost like a miniature dragon.

'Is it Monday or Tuesday?'

George looked round, but the rest of the queue had either filed out again into the other end of the Bedding Department, like Mum and Rosie, or were still mesmerised by Red Riding Hood and the wolf. There was no-one else in the cave apart from Sleeping Beauty looking very dead, and the Prince with the sleepy eyes. And the snakes and toads and the lizards stuck to the cardboard walls. And the sparkly lizard puffing out white smoke.

'Or Wednesday or Thursday?'

'It's Saturday,' George heard himself say. Then he felt ridiculous and looked round to see if anyone had noticed him talking to himself.

'Saturday, Monday, Friday, Tuesday. They're all the same to me.'

A prickly feeling ran up and down George's back. The words seemed to be coming from the sparkly lizard. A talking lizard! This was the best thing in the Grotto! Even better than the puffs of smoke. He would have to tell Tom about it, but would Tom believe him?

'George!' Mum was shouting to him from the Bedding Department.

'Coming,' said George. But his feet wouldn't let

him. He felt rooted there, staring at the fantastic little lizard who could talk and blow white smoke through its nostrils.

'Oh, I'm so *bored*,' groaned the lizard. 'You'd never believe how boring it is, scuttling up and down these dreary cardboard walls, day after day, and everyone staring and saying "Urgh," and "Yuk," and babies screaming, and Mums moaning about their feet and gasping for air and cups of tea.'

'What makes you talk?' asked George in a very low voice so that no-one would notice him talking to a lizard. He was amazed by the lizard's vocabulary. A rich aunt had given Rosie a talking doll but it had only said 'Change me' and 'I've got a wet nappy.'

George's voice must have been too low, for the lizard ignored his question, and went on:

'A cardboard cave in the Carpet and Bedding Department of Boddis & Geerings is really no place for a dragon.'

'A DRAGON!' exclaimed George, so loudly he felt the whole Grotto must have heard. 'But there aren't such things. Only in fairy stories,' he added in a whisper.

'Oh, don't be ridiculous,' said the dragon impatiently. 'What did you think I was? Just another plastic lizard, stuck to the cardboard walls with a blob of glue?'

George wondered how it could possibly have got there, but before he had time to ask, the dragon said: 'Is there any room in your pocket?'

George felt in his anorak pocket. There were three shrivelled conkers, a marble, two gritty pennies, a bubblegum wrapper, three bits of Lego and a piece of plasticine, hairy with fluff.

'George! I shan't tell you again!' Mum was losing her patience.

The dragon didn't wait for George to reply. George watched astonished as it unfolded two wings like golden fans, fluttered on to his shoulder, and, with silver claws outstretched, scurried down his anorak into his pocket.

Mum was pulling at his arm.

'George, for goodness' sake!' she exclaimed, dragging him down the last tunnel and out again into the world of beds and wardrobes and matting. 'Haven't you seen enough?'

Chapter 3

The light made George blink. It was like coming out of the pictures on a sunny day, only worse because just for a moment he'd felt as if he really had been in a strange and magical land where dragons had golden wings and could speak, and now he was back in the Bedding Department of Boddis & Geerings with the carpets, the quilts and the beds priced at £350, and Rosie hiccupping in her buggy. If he felt in his pocket now there would be just the conkers and the gritty pennies, the marble and the bubblegum wrapper, the bits of Lego and the hairy pieces of plasticine. And although he was so certain he must have imagined the dragon in the Grotto, because he couldn't bear the disappointment of finding out for sure he didn't dare put his hand in his pocket.

But if he had looked down at his anorak he would have seen tiny looped threads there where they had been pulled by silver claws.

George had just reached the top of the stairs when there came a muffled sound from his pocket: something complaining about the heat, the grit and the fluff.

Mum was walking up the stairs backwards,

dragging up the push-chair with Rosie in it hiccuping still. Could George have imagined that sound? His hand crept into his pocket. Something wriggly and scaly was still there, breathing hot air against his hand. It couldn't be true! Downstairs, perhaps, behind the faded red curtain, but not here among the beads and the belts and the scarves, and the smell of soap.

And then he realised that if it were true, if he really did have a real live dragon in his pocket, it was going to have to be the biggest secret he had ever had to keep. Because now he had it, he couldn't bear the thought of losing it. If Mum discovered it when they got home, she would jump on a chair and call Dad, and Dad would say they would have to give it to a zoo. But even a zoo didn't seem the right place for a dragon. Where did dragons live?

'Don't just stand there dreaming,' puffed Mum. 'Here, hold this,' and she gave George the carrier bag with a packet of washing powder in it and a wrapped loaf.

George walked along the shiny wet pavement, but he felt that only half of him was there. His feet didn't seem to be touching the ground.

'I've got to slip in here to get your Dad a nice bit of fish for his tea,' said Mum. 'Hold on to the buggy and keep your eye on Rosie. And watch that cabbage,' she added as she disappeared into the fish shop.

George wondered how to keep his secret. The dragon would have to be fed, but what did dragons eat? He would have to ask it. But how would he feed it without anyone noticing? How would he talk to it without anyone hearing? Suddenly he remembered Charlie. Charlie had been George's make-believe friend before Rosie was born. He'd turned up mostly at mealtimes when there were fish fingers or treacle pudding. 'Charlie wants some too,' he had said, and Mum had given him two helpings, one for himself and one for Charlie, and then George had eaten Charlie's helping too. Charlie would have to stay in George's pocket, out of sight, and George would spoon his helping down to him when no-one was looking. Dad was usually behind the newspaper anyway, and Mum preoccupied with shovelling revolting soupy stuff into Rosie. And if he called the dragon Charlie no-one would wonder why he was appearing to talk to himself. They would just take it for granted that Charlie had come back from wherever it was he had gone to when Rosie was born.

George was telling the secret in his pocket why he would have to be called Charlie when Mum came out of the fish shop, her woollen headscarf askew and falling sideways off her head.

'Oh, I clean forgot,' she said, ramming the packet of fish into her carrier bag, 'that dreadful Miss Prosser has asked us upstairs to tea this afternoon. It went right out of my mind.'

Miss Prosser! George had forgotten about her! What would *she* say if she discovered that George was keeping a pet dragon downstairs?

They set off for home, heads down against the rain,

Mum's umbrella dripping, Rosie grizzling beneath the plastic hood, her lap piled up with shopping, George with a packet of soap powder and a sliced loaf in a carrier bag in one hand, the other hand guarding his amazing secret.

Chapter 4

'I live in harf a howse,' George had written in his News Book that week at school. 'Me and my Dad, he works at the Coop, and Mum and Rosie and Pudding our cat. We live in the bottom of it and there is a landing lady and her name is Miss Prosser and she lives in the top of it. She is orlways moning about something like Pudding has eaten harf her marmerlade cake. She has cerled up yellow hair. Mum says that yellow is not reel.'

When he'd finished writing Mrs Trimble had come round with a red felt pen and underlined all the words he'd spelt wrongly, like 'harf' and 'howse' and 'marmerlade' and put a line between the two o's of Coop. He had to accept that Mrs Trimble was better at spelling than he was, though it was hard to believe when she spelt words like 'harf' h-a-l-f. But there was one word he knew she was wrong about. She had underlined 'landing lady' and written 'landlady' above it in her neat red writing. George had wanted to say that 'landlady' didn't make any sense at all; 'landing lady' did. If Mrs Trimble had been in their house she would know that Miss Prosser seemed to live on the landing. She hovered there, a tall, thin shape in her silky dress, calling over the banisters when they came in from school or shopping.

'Mrs Bunting dear, can I have a word?' Miss Prosser asked Mum for as many 'words' as Dad asked for cups of tea. They were either to do with Pudding or the front doorstep.

'Do try to keep it scrubbed, Mrs Bunting dear. First impressions are *so* important.' To encourage Mum Miss Prosser was always giving her tokens and vouchers she'd cut out from her magazines advertising 5p or 10p off polishes and scouring powders with energetic-sounding names like WHIZZO and SUD-ZO and ZING. Mum never used them; she said just reading the names made her feel tired.

Or Mum would climb the stairs wearily to be shown a newly baked cake with the inside scooped out, or a dead mouse in one of Miss Prosser's shiny high-heeled shoes. Pudding obviously thought Miss Prosser valued dead mice as much as he did, and that her marmalade cakes were her way of saying 'thank you'. He was a clever cat. He could open their doors by jumping up, hanging on to the handle, pulling it down and swinging in with it as it glided open. This was useful when they couldn't be bothered to get up and open the door for him, and as cats are always on the wrong side of a door, that was most of the time. But Pudding didn't just open the doors downstairs where the Buntings lived: he opened Miss Prosser's too and he seemed to prefer hers because inviting smells of chicken or hot marmalade cake were always wafting through the cracks and down the stairs.

'It's really too bad,' Miss Prosser would complain. 'I'd only turned my back for a moment.' And on particularly bad days it was 'that cat will have to go. I distinctly remember when I advertised the downstairs flat I added "No animals, caged birds only", but as a special concession I allowed you to keep Pudding. But this can't go on, Mrs Bunting dear, it really can't go on.'

Not much of the carpet showed in the Buntings' flat. It was always strewn with something. When they got home that afternoon from the Fairy Grotto they had

23

to pick their way between bits of Lego, a dolls' plastic tea-set, something sad knitted in grey wool with the stuffing leaking out, and a lopsided slipper with no toe. There was only one chair that wasn't overflowing with ironing and Mum collapsed into it.

'Mrs Bunting dear,' came the voice from the landing, 'you haven't forgotten I've invited you all up to tea this afternoon, have you?'

Is a dragon an animal? George wondered as they lumbered up Miss Prosser's staircase with its sparkling white paint. Rosie was clambering up on all fours like a crab, with toys to keep her amused spilling out of her pockets. Mum came last with Rosie's high-chair, plastic apron and unbreakable plate and mug. Charlie was still in George's pocket. He knew it was risky taking him up to tea with Miss Prosser, but he could think of no safe place to leave him.

Chapter 5

Miss Prosser was waiting for them on the landing in her best mauve silk dress and her pale mauve shoes to match. Mum was still wearing her old brown skirt fastened with one of Rosie's nappy-pins where the zip had broken, and her boring old shoes with the flat heels and the grease blobs on the toe.

Miss Prosser showed them into her sitting room. It was the first time George had seen it and he realised he had never seen a room so neat and sparkling before.

'Let me take your anorak, George dear,' said Miss Prosser, 'you do look hot!'

'No, thank you,' said George quickly. 'I'm quite cold really,' which was a stupid thing to say when his cheeks were burning from the excitement of having a real live dragon in his pocket.

'Well then, you'd better sit in that chair by the fire,' said Miss Prosser, and George sat down on the edge of an armchair patterned with blue pansies, with a lacy square over the back, and two more lacy squares over the arms, and hoped Charlie was going to be no trouble.

Miss Prosser had laid out some books for Rosie to look at while she went to make the tea. Mum sank down on the pansy-patterned sofa, grabbed Rosie, set her firmly on her lap and said in a voice that didn't sound like hers: 'Oh, look at this picture book that Miss Prosser had when she was a little girl! *Isn't* it pretty!'

Miss Prosser a little girl? She couldn't have been, thought George. She must surely have been born with tight yellow curls and a silky mauve dress: as tall and thin as a tube.

Rosie was squirming about on the sofa like a slithery fish, showing no interest at all in the picture book.

George sat stiffly on the edge of his chair, cupping his hand firmly over his pocket so that Charlie couldn't slither out, but with his fingers a bit apart to let some air through. He wondered whether he'd be able to manage to swallow any tea.

'Don't sit so near that fire, George,' Mum said in her normal voice. 'You'll scorch.'

Miss Prosser trundled in tea on a trolley. The plates were thin and delicate and covered with flowery sprigs. On the two large plates were rounds of lacy paper, one piled with the smallest sandwiches George had ever seen, cut into triangles with no crusts, and on the other was a cherry cake. On the tea-pot sat a lady doll in a woollen skirt in different coloured stripes. Rosie, scrambling over the sofa, tried to grab it.

Miss Prosser poured out weak tea into the rose-sprigged cups.

'Well now, isn't this cosy?' she said, placing the tea-cups and matching rose-sprigged plates on wobbly tables with lace cloths on them. Miss Prosser seemed fond of lace, thought George. The cups were just low enough for Rosie to seize. George took a Marmite sandwich.

Mum looked for Rosie, to seize her before she could seize the cups, but she had vanished. They found her behind Miss Prosser's chair, winding herself up in black cotton, her mouth full of buttons. Miss Prosser's mending basket had reels of cottons graded into all colours of the rainbow; needles and pins in neat packets, assorted thimbles, a tape-measure carefully wound, not strewn in a tangled mass like Mum's, and cards of press-studs in shining rows. All of it now lay scattered over Miss Prosser's fleecy white rug.

'Where are we?' The suddenness of the muffled voice from George's pocket made him jump. The weak tea slopped into his saucer. George gripped his tea-cup. Had anyone heard?

But Mum and Miss Prosser were behind Miss Prosser's chair, scraping back the contents of the mending basket.

'Having tea with Miss Prosser,' whispered George into his pocket. His voice was muffled by the Marmite sandwich in his mouth which seemed like a ball of wool that wouldn't go down. 'You've got to keep quiet because she doesn't approve of animals, only birds in cages, where they can't get into mischief.'

Mum was looking hot now, and her hair was

falling over her eyes. Miss Prosser's was still in tight, neat yellow rolls. Mum encased Rosie firmly in her high-chair, enveloped her in the plastic apron, put one of Miss Prosser's dainty sandwiches on Rosie's unbreakable plate and poured some milk into her unbreakable mug.

'Well, this is fun!' said Miss Prosser again with a smile that didn't seem quite real. George watched it set on her face, reminding him of the gnomes in the Grotto, and then fade as she watched Rosie peel open the Marmite sandwich, pull lumps off it, drop them in her milk, dabble her hand in the mug, pull out a milk-sodden lump, squeeze it like a sponge over her tray, and drop it in her plastic apron pocket.

'I don't think Rosie cares for the Marmite sandwich,' Miss Prosser said. 'Shall we try her with a little piece of cherry cake?'

Rosie dived at the cherry cake like a hungry bird, pulled out all the cherries, piled them in her mouth at one go, rubbed the rest of the cake between her hands until it had turned to crumbs, and then, with outstretched arms, shot the crumbs all over the floor.

'Oh Rosie,' wailed Mum. And Miss Prosser rushed out to her kitchen for her dustpan and brush.

Chapter 6

'I'm bored down here in the dark,' grumbled Charlie from the depths of George's pocket.

George grabbed a slice of cherry cake while Miss Prosser was out of the room and broke off a piece for Charlie.

'George! You should have waited till Miss Prosser offered you a slice,' whispered Mum, trying to scrape up the crumby mess on Rosie's tray with her tea-knife. She hauled Rosie out of her chair and dabbed her hands on a screwed-up paper napkin as Miss Prosser swept up the cake crumbs.

'Cherry cake is disgusting!' Charlie's voice was muffled and thick with crumbs, and crumbs and cherries were shot up in a fountain from George's pocket, and lay sprinkled round his feet. Any minute now Charlie would be clambering out of George's pocket, running up his anorak, spreading his golden wings and landing on Miss Prosser's head. Miss Prosser would have hysterics and Charlie would dart about among the tight yellow curls turning them into a bird's nest and blowing smoke into her ears. The thought of it made George feel very hot. He sat on the edge of his chair with his knees pressed tightly together wondering when it would be time to go.

'Can't you go to sleep, Charlie?' George whispered into his pocket. 'If Miss Prosser discovers you she'll put you in a cage.'

'I thought I'd swept round there,' said Miss Prosser, brushing up the crumbs and cherries round George's feet.

'Oh George, what a mess!' said Mum. 'You're as bad as Rosie. You should be ashamed of yourself, a big boy like you.'

'I see our little Master Make-believe is back with us again,' said Miss Prosser to Mum as she sank back into her chair. She spoke out of the corner of her mouth, screwing up one side of her face in a rather obvious wink in George's direction.

'Oh, you don't need to tell me. He's been jabbering away to Charlie all the way home from the shops,' said Mum, in the way grown-ups have, pretending you're deaf or just not there. 'We thought when Rosie came along that would put a stop to it.'

'Yes,' Miss Prosser said, 'I would have thought so. One expects very young children to live in a make-believe world, but children of George's age should have grown out of it.'

George would like to have said, so should grown-ups of her age. Her room was full of make-believe things. There were make-believe plastic tulips which looked stupid in December, and make-believe fish swimming about in a make-believe ship's wheel among make-believe seaweed. Even the tea-pot had a make-believe doll on it. Surely Miss Prosser was too old for dolls. And there was the make-believe coal stuck to the bottom of the electric fire with the make-believe flickery flame which didn't give off any heat. Only the bar above it was hot, and it seemed to be getting hotter all the time.

'You look a bit warm there, George dear,' said Miss Prosser. 'Are you sure you wouldn't like to take off your coat?'

Why couldn't they go on pretending he wasn't there? thought George, shaking his head.

'Well, I'll turn off the fire then,' and she clicked off the switch, but the cardboard coal still flickered its make-believe flame.

'Well now,' said Miss Prosser, sipping her untouched tea, which by then must have been quite cold, 'I thought we could have a little chat about Pudding.' She was doing her best to ignore Rosie who was wheeling Matchbox cars up and down her legs.

So that's why she's asked us all up to tea, thought George.

'I have a friend,' went on Miss Prosser, 'called Letty Parsons. She lives in the country – much the most suitable place for a cat. She's plagued by mice, poor dear, so I told her about Pudding and what an excellent mouser he is, but such a trial to all of us, and we both agreed it would be the best thing all round if he goes to live with her.'

'Oh, he can't do that!' cried Mum indignantly. 'He's our cat, and he's not a trial to us.'

George liked Mum to get angry, when he wasn't the cause of it.

'Well, I can't have animals roaming all over the house,' said Miss Prosser, getting angry too. She made it sound as if the house were being invaded by escaped circus animals. George quailed at the thought of what she would do on finding a dragon on her landing.

'I suggest you change the door handles,' said Mum. 'He hasn't learned to turn knobs yet.'

'I really don't see why I should go to all that trouble,' retorted Miss Prosser.

'Well, you'll just have to put bolts on your doors, then,' suggested Mum.

'What! Barricade myself into my own house? Whatever next!'

What did happen next put an end to the argument,

the tea party and everything else, for white smoke started to curl up steadily from George's pocket; not little puffs, but clouds of it, enveloping George entirely. Miss Prosser screamed, Mum screamed, and Rosie screamed. And then something cold and white and wet was being thrown over George. As it trickled down his neck, over his sleeves, down his legs and into his shoes, he realised that Miss Prosser had thrown the contents of the milk jug over him.

'Oh George!' cried Mum, trembling, 'I told you not to sit so near that fire. Why don't you ever listen?'

She was hauling him out of the door and hustling him down the stairs with one hand, and the wailing Rosie with the other, while Miss Prosser stood on the landing, flapping the smoke away with her paper napkin, muttering to herself, because no-one else was there to listen:

'I can't understand it. I simply can't understand it. It's a real mystery. I'd turned the fire off. It wasn't hot. It wasn't even warm.'

Chapter 7

'You won't want much supper after all that tea,'
Mum said, banging saucepans around in the kitchen,
getting supper ready. She was still carrying on her
argument with Miss Prosser.

George had had to strip off all his clothes after Miss
Prosser had thrown the milk over him, and have a
bath. Mum had put the clothes in the sink to soak
while he'd put his pyjamas on ready for bed. Charlie
was curled up in his dressing-gown pocket, asleep,
George hoped. Rosie was in bed and Dad was grunt-
ing answers at Mum from behind the evening paper.

'The cheek of it!' said Mum, slapping Dad's bit of
fish on to a plate, and a dollop of scrambled egg on to
George's. 'Miss Prosser getting it all arranged for
Pudding to go and live with that Letty somebody-or-
other in the country. Anyone would think he was *her*
cat.' She seemed more cross about Pudding, George
thought, than about Miss Prosser throwing the milk
at him. He could feel Charlie squirming and wriggling in the pocket of his dressing-gown. He realised
he hadn't yet discovered what dragons like to eat.

'Charlie wants some scrambled egg too,' George
said, hoping Charlie preferred scrambled egg to
cherry cake.

'Well, Charlie will have to go without,' said Mum. 'I'm not cooking another thing tonight.'

While Mum was in the kitchen fetching the tomato sauce George spooned scrambled egg down to Charlie in his pocket.

'Isn't it about time Charlie made himself scarce?' muttered Dad from behind his paper, his mouth full of fish and boiled potato.

George soon found that Charlie didn't care for scrambled egg either. He flung it out of George's pocket in disgust and it rolled around on his lap in little rubbery balls.

'Oh George,' wailed Mum, coming in from the kitchen, 'you're as bad as Rosie, throwing your scrambled egg all over the floor. Get off to bed, quick.' She grovelled under the table, scraping up the

mess with a spoon. 'I've had just about all I can take for one day.'

What was he going to do with Charlie? George wondered as he cleaned his teeth. Now that the first excitement had worn off, George was beginning to realise that having a dragon for a pet, even one small enough to fit in your pocket, wasn't like keeping a cat or a budgie. Pudding wasn't fussy about food, nor did he blow smoke out of his nostrils when he got bored. And having a landing lady upstairs who allowed only caged birds in her house made everything worse. Caged birds! Perhaps he could persuade Charlie to live in a cage. He would be safer from Pudding there, too. He would ask Mum to buy a budgie and then he would let the budgie fly away and Charlie could live in the cage where he couldn't get into mischief. But Charlie didn't think much of the idea and said he had no intention of being caged up like a budgie. 'Being cooped up day after day in that dingy Grotto was bad enough,' and he scurried all over George's bed, pulling up the threads of the bedspread with his tiny silver claws.

'Do dragons go to bed?' George asked, climbing in, 'or do they just lie down in their caverns like crocodiles, with unblinking eyes, pretending they're a log?'

'Yes, of course they go to bed,' said Charlie, slithering his scaly body under the covers and curling up on George's chest.

'You'll have to stay there out of sight, then, till

Mum's been in to kiss me goodnight and Dad's read me a story,' George warned. He much preferred Dad to read his bedtime story. Mum usually fell asleep over it. She would get to the really exciting part where the Giant was roaring his "Fee, fi, fo, fum," and then she'd start to yawn, and her voice would go all droney. Her eyelids would droop and her head would fall forwards. George would prod her and she would jerk her head up and say: 'Where was I? Oh yes, "fo, fum." But by then the Giant wasn't frightening any more. Dad was better because he did a different voice for each character, and when he did the Giant he roared out the "FEE, FI, FO, FUM!" so that Pudding, who sometimes lay on his bed, would leap off with his fur on end.

'Now tell me what dragons *really* like to eat,' George asked Charlie. He could feel Charlie's claws sinking like pins through his pyjama jacket and would have preferred Charlie to have chosen some other place to bed down for the night.

'Not scrambled egg or cherry cake, that's for sure,' was all that George could get from Charlie.

What would take a dragon's fancy, wondered George dreamily: sausages? fish fingers? jelly? apple dumplings?

When Mum came in to kiss him goodnight, George and a small rolled-up mound beneath the covers were fast asleep.

Chapter 8

George was woken by a crash: a tray with two cups of tea being dropped on his bedroom floor. Mum, who had just made the tea for herself and Dad, had looked in on George to see if he was awake. She was now standing on his chair, clutching her faded blue dressing-gown tightly below her knees, her eyes riveted on George's pillow.

'Don't move, George!' She spoke the words through clenched teeth, hardly moving her lips, like Miss Prosser the day before when she hadn't wanted George to think she was talking about him.

'Whatever you do, George, don't move!' And then louder: 'Dad! Fetch the tooth-mug, quick, and the postcard of Cleethorpes.' The tooth-mug and the picture postcard that Aunt Truda had sent them three years ago from Cleethorpes were kept high up on the bathroom shelf, wedged between the Vaseline and a murky bottle with brown smudges and what looked like 'Btimoadag Siveoetabbf' scrawled across the label in spiky writing, used by Mum for their coughs. The postcard and the tooth-mug were kept there as an ever-ready method of trapping outsize spiders and removing them safely to the garden.

'Mrs Bunting dear, is anything the matter down

there?' Miss Prosser leant over the banisters in her pink quilted house-coat with its lacy collar and cuffs, her yellow hair in rollers. 'I thought I heard a crash.'

'Just dropped the tea tray,' shouted up Dad from the hall. 'Nothing for you to worry about.'

When he got back with the tooth-mug and the postcard Mum was still rooted to George's chair.

'There's some sort of creature on George's pillow,' she hissed through clenched teeth.

'Well I'll be blowed!' exclaimed Dad. 'If it isn't a lizard!' He was amazed. 'A rare one too by the look of it. One thing's for sure, it's too big to go under the tooth-mug.'

'Well, don't just stand there,' said Mum just standing there. 'What if it bites George?'

'Lizards don't bite,' said Dad, turning George's waste-bin upside down over Charlie so that old brown apple cores, bits of Lego and pencil shavings scattered over his pillow. As he looked around for something large and flat enough to slide underneath, George held his breath, wondering what he was going to do with Charlie. Dad was wondering too.

'Well, that's a relief!' gasped Mum, collapsing into a heap on the chair. Now that Dad had assured her lizards were harmless, she seemed to be getting over the shock. 'Wherever could such a thing have come from? We'd better get Miss Prosser to ring up the Council to get the house fumigated. Fleas and beetles in the house are bad enough, but lizards!'

'Can I keep it?' asked George, suddenly. They had discovered half his secret, but not the part that really mattered, the magical part. They thought George was just a rather unusual type of lizard. With his wings folded up he looked like one.

'*Keep* it?' Mum was astonished. 'Whatever do you want to keep it for?'

'Because it would be a different sort of pet,' said George. 'I'd be able to show it to my friends at school. They've only got boring things like guinea-pigs and mice and sleepy old tortoises that stay in their shells all the time.'

But George knew he wouldn't tell his friends, even Tom. Charlie was the most exciting secret George had ever had and he wasn't going to let anyone else share it.

'Whatever would Miss Prosser say?' said Mum. 'You know she doesn't approve of pets in the house. We have enough trouble with Pudding.'

'But it wouldn't be any trouble,' persisted George. 'It could live in my pocket and Miss Prosser would never know. And it's so small it wouldn't eat much.'

'And that's another thing,' said Mum, 'what's it going to eat, and who's going to feed it, I'd like to know. I've got my hands full getting meals for you three and Pudding without worrying about a lizard.'

'Are you going to keep this thing or not?' interrupted Dad, still holding the waste-bin over Charlie. They could hear him scuttling about underneath, getting cross. In a minute he'll start blowing out smoke, thought George, and then what?

'I'll look after him and I'll feed him,' said George. 'I'll soon find something he likes.'

But it was going to take longer than George thought to discover what dragons like to eat. Charlie had already rejected cherry cake and scrambled egg. Dad looked up 'lizard' in the dictionary.

'"Lizard: four-legged scaly reptile with long tail",' Dad read out. 'It doesn't tell you what they eat.'

'Perhaps they eat the same sort of thing as birds,'

suggested George, remembering Charlie's wings.

'Well you're not catching me digging up worms this weather,' Mum retorted.

'When I was a boy,' Dad said, 'and it was too cold for the birds to find their own food, we used to put hunks of old cheese on the bird table, and dobs of dripping, and bacon rinds left over from breakfast, and even rotten apples.'

Rotten apples and dobs of dripping? It didn't sound the sort of diet you could offer a dragon with rainbow scales and silver claws: as out of place as porridge at a banquet.

'Some boys' Mums even cooked special food for the bird table . . .' Dad went on.

'Who's got time to cook for birds these days, I should like to know,' Mum interrupted.

'They used to boil up mounds of gluey rice and potatoes in their skins and then they chopped it all around with lumps of dripping and stale old scones and cake, and topped it all off with a fish-head the cat had left.'

'It's enough to make your stomach heave just listening to it, let alone having to cook it,' complained Mum.

'How about mealworms?' suggested Dad. 'My best school chum used to breed them. He'd punch some holes in the lid of an old cocoa tin . . . No, on second thoughts, better not.'

I know what second thoughts Dad's having, thought George. He's thinking that keeping a lizard's going to be enough trouble without the place being overrun with mealworms. Any minute now he's going to say: 'Well, I give up.'

'Well, I give up,' said Dad. 'It's your lizard.'

That day George offered Charlie all the most delicious things he could think of, including the cheese and onion crisps still left in the bag from Friday, to the treacle pudding and custard Mum dished up for dinner. But Charlie rejected them all. By the evening he still hadn't discovered what Charlie liked to eat.

Chapter 9

'You're a funny sort of dragon,' George said to Charlie in bed that night as he lay curled up on George's chest. He wanted to add that he thought him just the slightest bit boring too, but didn't want to hurt Charlie's feelings.

'Why?' asked Charlie, his feelings hurt already.

'Well, you aren't a bit like the dragons in books.'

'What are they like?' asked Charlie, swishing his tail crossly against George's neck. His scales were getting scratchy: it was like sharing your bed with a saucepan-scourer, George thought.

'Sort of exciting, and about a hundred times bigger than you,' ventured George. 'They're huge scaly monsters with spines down their backs where your little gold bumps are, and they fly high up in the clouds. I've only seen you fly once when you fluttered on to my shoulder in the Grotto, and that wasn't proper flying. You haven't even fluttered since then. No-one even knows you have wings except me. Proper dragons fight knights on white horses and gobble up Princesses. You don't even gobble up treacle pudding.'

'I can breathe fire,' Charlie said.

'Not proper fire, only little puffs of steamy smoke.'

And then he realised he'd really hurt Charlie's feelings because the little dragon started huffing and puffing out his white smoke until the bedroom was quite thick with it and insufferably hot.

'Your scales are pretty,' George said quickly, trying to make up for what he'd said, hoping the smoke would soon evaporate. 'I like the glittery bits and your silvery claws and your ruby eyes. I just wish you were a bit more magic, that's all.'

'What makes you think I'm not magic?' asked Charlie through the smoke.

'Well, you've never done anything magical.'

'You've never asked me,' Charlie replied.

'You mean you can do magic?' George's eyes were wide with amazement.

'I could try,' Charlie said. 'What would you like to be changed into?'

George wondered. He'd often thought about it, especially when Mrs Trimble had called him up to her desk because he'd got all his sums wrong. Sometimes, on wet mornings when he had sloshed through the puddles on his way to school he had thought what fun it would be to be an elephant: to suck up all the puddles through your trunk and shoot the water out again in great gushing jets all over Mrs Throgmorton as she stood at the school gates in her bright red coat and her shiny gold hair waving goodbye to Fenella.

A dinosaur would be even better. You could let people slide down your back: not just your friends but all the tired-looking people who trundled trollies round the Co-op and looked as if they had never had any fun in the whole of their lives; and the old tramp who slept under newspapers on the bench in the park. They would all clamber on to your head, throwing their shopping and the old newspapers into the air, and then they would whoosh down your neck and your back, up and over your humps, and drop, screaming and bellowing with laughter, off the end of your tail.

And all the awful people like Miss Prosser and Fenella Throgmorton you could simply Hoover up and swallow whole. But perhaps you couldn't. Hadn't Mrs Trimble told them that there weren't any people in the world when dinosaurs were lumbering around in their steamy swamps? And anyway a dinosaur's mouth was quite small. Even if you managed to swallow Fenella she would be dreadfully indigestible, and Miss Prosser would get lodged halfway down.

And how do you get through a door if you're a dinosaur or an elephant? It would get a bit tedious if every time you wanted to walk through one you got wedged in it as tight as a cork in a bottle, Mum and Dad heaving and tugging your head or your trunk, with neighbours from all down the street having to clamber in through the window to push you from behind. And on the landing Miss Prosser would be hovering and moaning: 'This can't go on, Mrs Bunting dear, it simply can't go on.'

What about a giant golden eagle? To be able to

soar high above the clouds where there weren't any Miss Prossers or sums to bother you? But how long would Charlie's magic last? What if it faded while you were swooping thousands of metres above sheer jagged cliffs or a stormy, foaming sea and you dropped like a stone? What then?

Then George thought of Mum: it seemed safer. Perhaps Charlie could try out his magic on her and turn all those awful old brown clothes done up with safety pins into something pretty and frilly.

Charlie thought he could manage that.

'What about her wellingtons?' asked George. 'Could you change them into shiny black shoes with tall spiky heels and glittery bits on the toe?'

'Well,' said Charlie, 'if I gave her a frilly frock I could hardly leave her wearing wellingtons.'

But what if Mum came to meet him from school and Charlie's spell had only half worked? An alarming picture formed in his mind: Mrs Throgmorton and all the other Mums standing there, and all his friends swarming out of the school gates, and Mum in a fairy-tale frock and wellingtons, clutching a carrier bag.

'Anyway,' said George, 'as you're only a learner and you haven't done any magic yet, perhaps it would be better to practise on something that isn't alive, just in case you don't get it right.' He could see that Charlie's feelings were hurt again so he went on quickly: 'What about my Lego dumper truck? See if you can turn it into a real one. Not a full-size one – it wouldn't fit in the bedroom, but big enough for me to ride in and scoop up all my rubbish with it so Mum wouldn't need to keep moaning any more about all the mess.'

Charlie said he'd try, so they got out of bed and George set the Lego dumper truck in the middle of the carpet and he and Charlie crouched down side by side. Charlie huffed and puffed his white steamy smoke at it but when the smoke cleared the dumper

truck was still made of Lego and still as small as it had been before all the huffing and puffing.

'If you were about a hundred times bigger it might work,' said George sadly. 'And fairy-tale dragons breathe fire,' he reminded Charlie, 'that's why nothing's happening. Try blowing out flames.'

Charlie huffed and puffed some more until they couldn't see across the room for smoke, but no flames came.

'I don't know how you expect me to breathe fire, and grow huge, and fly up in the clouds fighting knights and gobbling up Princessess,' snapped Charlie, suddenly cross again, 'when I haven't had a bite to eat.'

'That's not my fault,' said George, cross now too. 'I've offered you all sorts of nice things but you just spit them out.'

'Cherry cake, scrambled egg, treacle pudding? You call that *food*? Why can't you find something I can *really* get my teeth into?'

'And why can't you tell me what dragons really eat? If you truly are a dragon, you should *know*.'

'How could I know?' retorted Charlie, flashing his ruby eyes. 'Nobody knows what they like to eat until they're given it. Did Rosie know she wanted that revolting, pulpy, soupy stuff until it was shovelled into her mouth?'

George had to admit he didn't suppose she did. He'd often wondered how she could bear to eat it at all.

'But what did you eat before I rescued you from the Grotto at Boddis & Geerings?' asked George.

'Eat? What would you expect me to eat,' snapped Charlie, 'in a make-believe palace with cardboard walls, and rubber snakes and plastic toads?'

'But what about *before* you were in the Grotto?' persisted George. 'You must have eaten something then.'

Charlie glowered at him with his fiery eyes. He said nothing for a long time, and then he rolled his eyes upwards as though he were trying to remember.

'There wasn't a "before",' he said at last.

'Oh,' said George. He felt there was still a lot he didn't understand. Who had taught Charlie how to talk? And how had he got into the Grotto in the first place? Boddis & Geerings sold all sorts of things from beads to beds, from duvets to darning wool; but it wasn't the sort of shop where you would say casually after you'd bought your card of elastic, 'Oh, by the way, have you any dragons in stock?'

But Charlie was swishing his tail angrily, and making snorting noises through his nostrils, and was clearly in no mood for answering questions.

So they climbed back into bed. But instead of settling down on George's chest, Charlie scrambled down to the bottom of the bed and curled himself into a sulky knot.

Chapter 10

'It'll eat when it's hungry enough,' said Mum next morning, slapping Christmas cake together in the mixing bowl. George's class had been given the day off school and George was sitting at the table with Charlie on his shoulder, waiting to scrape out the bowl. Pudding, crouched at the end of the table, had his greedy eyes on the mixture too. Rosie was in her high-chair chewing up the first Christmas card.

'What are you going to do with that creature when you go back to school tomorrow, I'd like to know?' Mum asked, tipping more flour and fruit into the bowl, the flour sprinkling over the table and the floor.

George didn't answer. He was making a fist witch to frighten Rosie. He clenched his fist tightly, twisted his wrist round till his thumb was resting on the table, pushed his thumb between his first and second fingers to make a tongue, picked out two currants from the packet on the table and poked them through the crack between his second and third fingers, on each side of his knuckles, to look like eyes. Then he took out his hanky to drape round his hand for the witch's cloak. Making a noise like a witch's cackle he wiggled the 'tongue' in Rosie's face to make his fist look like a Rosie-gobbling witch, and waited for her to scream. Rosie, her mouth full of chewed-up Christmas card, gave the 'witch' a passing glance, and grinned. George looked at his fist with his hanky wrapped round it; it didn't look much like a witch; it looked more like a ghost. A ghost! Himself covered in Mum's old torn-up sheet! All the excitement of finding Charlie and trying to find out what he liked to eat had put the dreaded Fancy Dress Party out of his mind. The witch's face collapsed, its currant eyes rolling over Rosie's tray. Rosie crammed them into her mouth to join the sodden Christmas card.

'If you're not careful,' Mum went on, 'Pudding will have that lizard for dinner.'

But George wasn't listening. He was thinking back to his conversation with Charlie in bed the night

before. Why hadn't he thought of it then? The thing he wanted most of all – to be transformed into something amazing for the Party! Mum couldn't do it for him; Dad couldn't either. But if only he could find out what dragons ate to make them magic, perhaps Charlie could! He could feel his heart beating very fast. He must find out soon.

'And another thing,' Mum was saying, dolloping in the last of the dried fruit. 'One of these days it's going to discover the stairs and go scuttling up to Miss Prosser's, and then what?'

George didn't have time to answer because at that moment Charlie decided to see if he liked raw Christmas cake. He slithered down George's jumper and plopped on to the kitchen table. But he got no further. Pudding sprang like a mouse-trap and seized Charlie's squirming scaly body between his teeth. Then, before Mum or George could grab him, he'd darted out of the kitchen with the struggling Charlie, streaked down the hall, through their open door and up Miss Prosser's gleaming white stairs. Her door, too, was open. On the eighth stair he stopped and crouched there, daring them to come closer, Charlie now dangling limply from Pudding's fat and whiskery jowls.

George remembered that Pudding put only dead creatures in Miss Prosser's shoes. Charlie looked very dead. Oh, why couldn't I have found out what dragons like to eat? George thought in despair. Then Charlie could have turned himself into something too

big for Pudding to eat. Now it was too late, and he would never be able to help him with the Fancy Dress costume.

'Stop him!' Mum cried out. 'If Pudding goes up there just once more he'll have to go to that Letty woman in the country.'

But George was more concerned for Charlie. If Pudding killed Charlie he wouldn't care if Pudding was sent to live with Letty Parsons. It would serve him right. He crept up the stairs slowly, silently, holding his breath, even though it was probably too late now to save Charlie: one stair . . . two stairs. Pudding crouched there, staring at him with his baleful yellow eyes, his cheeks bulging. If only Charlie weren't dead; if only he could save him in time: his one last hope. Three stairs . . . four stairs. But his one last hope still hung limply from between Pudding's jaws, and would soon be lying still and lifeless in Miss Prosser's shoe.

He made a grab at Pudding from the fourth stair but Pudding was too quick for him. He sprang up, shot up the last four stairs and through Miss Prosser's door, leaving George grabbing only the banister to stop himself falling down the stairs. He waited for Miss Prosser's shrieks. Mum couldn't bear to and went back to the kitchen to finish the Christmas cake. Too late now, she thought.

But no shrieks came; only the sound of a yowling Pudding and a furious scrabbling kerfuffle from Miss Prosser's landing. The next moment Pudding, with his fur on end like a toothbrush, hurled himself down the stairs, pursued by Charlie in a cloud of steamy smoke belching from his nostrils.

A moment later Miss Prosser emerged.

'Mrs Bunting dear,' came the voice from the landing. 'The rooms up here are full of steam. I should be glad if you could please remember to put the lids on your saucepans when you simmer.'

Chapter 11

'I've got to go to Tarringtons this afternoon,' Mum said at dinner time, trying to shovel pulpy mashed banana into Rosie's mouth while Rosie kept swivelling her head round so that the banana ended up, a tacky mess, in her hair.

'Oh, *why?*' George groaned. Tarringtons' coal-yard was surely the most boring, dismal place in the whole world.

'To pay the bill for the last load of coke,' Mum said, 'and order another.' The coke kept the kitchen stove burning and heated their water. Tarringtons delivered it in a lorry and tipped the coke down a chute to the coal-hole in the cellar. It was fun watching it hurtle down into the blackness, but he loathed being dragged along to the coal-yard.

'Do I *have* to come?' George whined.

'Yes, of course you have to come,' Mum said impatiently, whipping the dirty plates off the table and into the sink. 'Now help me get Rosie ready.'

There was the usual frantic search for Rosie's clothes. Rosie's drawer was even more of a jumble than George's: it was full of cotton sun-hats and matted, shrunken bootees that Rosie and George had worn as tiny babies. Mum heaped the whole lot on the floor and they rummaged together amongst the pile for Rosie's outdoor clothes.

'I don't *want* to go to Tarringtons,' George grumbled, delving through old woollen vests with holes in the hem where the nappy-pins had frayed them. 'I *hate* that dreary old coal-yard. *Why* do I have to?' Charlie was the only one enjoying himself, burrowing his way through Rosie's knitted cardigans and wriggling through the sleeves.

'Oh stop moaning, George, for goodness' sake!' said Mum, exasperated. 'And stop that creature running everywhere. He's dragging the threads with his claws.'

Mum found the leggings she was searching for at last and crammed everything back in the drawer.

'Can I take Charlie?' asked George, brightening up suddenly. 'And can we go to the sweet shop on the way?' He'd remembered he had to find what dragons like to eat.

Mum said he could as long as George made sure he stayed in his pocket. 'You don't want him darting into the road and disappearing under a bus. He's given us one fright too many as it is.'

'And can we go to Boddis & Geerings to look at the toys on the way back?'

'If there's time,' Mum said wearily.

It was always a cold wet dreary afternoon when they went to Tarringtons. Huge bleak sheds and great mountains of gloomy coal loomed out of the grey

December afternoon as they splashed their way through the sooty puddles and up the rickety steps to the Accounts Office. Inside, a sad, pale-faced woman with scraped-back hair sat behind a typewriter staring at the window. 'Merry Xmas' had been scrawled across it with silver glitter and blobs of cotton-wool were stuck to the pane.

George could feel Charlie fidgeting in his pocket.

'I know it's boring here, Charlie,' whispered George as Mum paid the bill, 'but we shan't have to stay long. We'll soon be at Boddis & Geerings and there'll be heaps and heaps of toys.' He felt a cheery warm glow just thinking of them all, and when they got home he'd got new things from the sweet shop to tempt Charlie with. Something he could really get his teeth into.

'Go and see if Rosie's all right,' Mum said to George. She'd left her at the bottom of the wooden steps, strapped into her push-chair. He found her trying to squirm out to reach a shining lump of coal that had rolled in a puddle by his feet. Before George could stop her she had grabbed it and stuffed it into her mouth in a frenzy of excitement.

'Oh Rosie, you can't eat coal!' George could hear himself sounding just like Mum. He fished out the coal from her mouth, got his hanky out, licked it and scrubbed round Rosie's mouth as Mum had so often done to him. It was when he put the hanky back in his pocket he realised something was wrong. Something that should have been there wasn't. He felt in his other pocket, in his trouser pockets, he felt round his neck, he swivelled his head round to peer over first one shoulder and then the other.

'Charlie, where are you hiding?'

And then, out of the corner of his eyes, he saw a flash of silver, a glitter of gold as something darted over the nearest mountain of coal and disappeared.

'Charlie!' George shouted, 'don't run off. We're going to Boddis & Geerings now to see the toys. And when we get home,' he added, 'I've got some new exciting things for you to eat.'

But from the mountain of coal there was now no sign of Charlie.

Chapter 12

George wondered what to do. Should he pretend not to care, and when Mum came down the steps, just walk off with her and Rosie, without looking back? It was what Mum did when he didn't come when she called him. When Charlie saw them going off to Boddis & Geerings without him he'd be sure to come scrambling back off the coal mountain and catch them up.

'Don't drag so, George,' Mum said as they splashed their way back through the murky puddles towards the shops. 'Don't you want to see the toys?'

George was hanging on to the push-chair, scuffing bits of coal with his shoe so that he would look to Charlie casual and not caring. But was Charlie following? Was he even noticing them, walking off as though they didn't care?

He sneaked a look over his shoulder. He was such a very little dragon and now it was getting dark he could so easily get lost. There was no sign of Charlie: no trickle of coal where Charlie might be slithering down: no flash of a silver claw, or a glowing ruby eye. Just mound after black mound, stretching away across the coal-yard, dank and still and fading away into the gloom, like crouching monsters lying in wait.

'Charlie's gone!' he blurted out, and found himself blundering back towards the coal heap where he'd last seen him, splashing his socks with sooty spray. His sudden fear of losing Charlie overcame his fear of the threatening gloom.

And now he was slipping and sliding over the coal as it slithered in streaming cascades beneath his scrunching shoes. He must find him.

'Charlie! Charlie!' he shouted into the darkening shadows, his legs sprawling out sideways as the tumbling heap gave way beneath him, his arms flying out to steady himself from falling.

Something was grabbing him by the collar and dragging him back, down to the ground.

'For goodness' sake, George!' Mum's voice was impatient. 'What *do* you think you're up to? You'll never find him in all that lot – it would be like looking for a needle in a haystack. I told you not to let him out of your pocket. Just look at you!' and she licked her hanky and started dabbing at his sooty socks.

The door of the Accounts Office opened, laying a band of yellow light down the wooden steps. The woman with the scraped-back hair peered out.

'Has the little boy lost something?' she asked.

'Only a lizard,' called back Mum, and the woman shrank back into her office, shuddering, as Mum dragged George by the arm and trundled him and Rosie in the buggy towards Boddis & Geerings.

The Toy Department was eye-blinkingly bright and

crowded with children with their Mums and Dads. It was hot and noisy with whirring train sets, bleeping computer games and clanking robots. Toy cars zoomed round plastic race-tracks and boxes of Sindy dolls stood stiffly in their boxes like sentries on duty. A fidgety queue was waiting by a plastic space rocket with flashing lights.

'What's the matter with you, George?' Mum asked him, exasperated. 'Don't you want to queue up for the space rocket? You've been pestering to come for weeks.'

George felt he wasn't really there at all. He was back at the coal-yard. It would be quite dark there now, apart from the yellow square of light from the Accounts Office window with its grubby blobs of cotton-wool snow. And soon that would be dark too. He could imagine Charlie crouching in the coal, shivering and lonely, or trying to get home, wandering helplessly along strange cold streets, blowing out little puffs of smoke to warm himself.

'Hi there, Chief!' A fat finger prodded George in the ribs. Mr Toogood, muffled up in a thick red scarf and tweed overcoat, beamed at him broadly. 'Great toys here!'

He's come to look at the robots, thought George gloomily, to get the finishing touches right for Tom's costume. Tom, at the head of the queue, was climbing into the rocket, flushed and proud, imagining himself the first astronaut to take off for Mars.

'Your Dad here, getting ideas for the Fancy Dress

Do?' Mr Toogood gave George a knowing wink. He was the sort of person who didn't really expect an answer, and if you gave one, didn't listen to it.

'He's at the Co-op,' George mumbled. For a wild moment he wondered if he could ask Mr Toogood to make him a costume. But you can't make proper costumes out of nothing and he hadn't any pocket money left to pay for it after buying Charlie's sweets.

Mum didn't notice Mr Toogood. She was diving at Rosie who was reaching out from her push-chair to seize a Sindy doll off the shelf and cram it in her mouth.

'What's up, Chief?' Why did Mr Toogood always have to call him that? Probably because he can't remember my name, George thought. 'You look as if you've found a penny and lost a pound!' He gave such a loud, explosive laugh it sent a spinning top whirring off the shelf. If only that was all I'd lost, thought George miserably.

'I haven't got anything to wear for the . . .' George began, suddenly bold, hoping Mr Toogood would take pity on him and make him a costume for nothing. But his voice trailed away. Mr Toogood wasn't listening. He was already pushing his way through the crowd of children to look at Tom showing off in the space rocket.

Mr Toogood's ideas didn't turn out all that good anyway, George thought crossly. Tom had made such a fuss about the tree-house his Dad had made back in the summer. He'd asked George and all his

other friends to come and admire it and they'd had a
Midnight Feast up there. It had been exciting plan-
ning it, hoarding up cakes and crisps and baked
beans beneath the bed. When the great night came
they had crept out of their houses without waking
their Mums and Dads and climbed up the swaying
rope ladder in the dark. But when they were all up
there, crouching in the branches, shivering and staring into inky blackness, they had wondered to themselves why they'd come. The cakes were stale and
dry, the crisps were soft and they couldn't find the tin
opener in the dark. They'd tried hard to persuade
themselves they were having fun. They had kept

saying: 'Isn't this great?' and 'Can't wait to do it again,' but when eventually one of them had been brave enough to say he wanted to get back to bed, they hadn't been able to scramble down the rope ladder fast enough.

'Can we go back to the coal-yard?' George asked Mum as she strapped Rosie more securely into her buggy.

'The coal-yard?' Mum almost shouted the words in her disbelief so that Mums and Dads and children turned their heads to stare.

'I just don't understand you, George. Every year you go on and on, wearing me down to bring you here to look at the toys, and every year you moan and whine and grumble about having to come with me to the coal-yard. Now I've lugged you and Rosie and the buggy and the shopping all the way up here and all you can think of is getting back to the coal-yard.'

'I want to go back and look for Charlie.' George's throat was feeling tight and lumpy and his eyes were pricking.

'You'll never find him now, my love,' Mum said more gently, 'I'm afraid he's gone for good. Come on,' she added, giving George a comforting hug and a wet kiss, 'Let's get home. I'm gasping for a cup of tea.'

Beside George's bed that night lay three unopened packets: a cellophane bag of peanut brittle, a packet of bubblegum, and a screwed-up paper bag of treacle toffee.

Chapter 13

For the next ten days leading up to the Fancy Dress Party George was inconsolable. Mum hardly mentioned Charlie, but Dad tried to cheer him up.

'Whoever finds him,' he said, 'will be sure to take him to the zoo. They'll be able to identify him there and will know what to feed him. And after Christmas we'll go along to the zoo and see if we can find him.'

After Christmas would be too late, thought George gloomily. It wasn't just that he missed Charlie and worried about him in that dismal coal-yard. There was now no hope of his going to the Fancy Dress Party in anything else but that dreadful old sheet. What had started as a small cloud of worry, which only appeared when he thought about it, and passed over when he forgot about it, now hung like a thundercloud as the day of the Party got nearer. At night he lay awake for hours, tossing and turning. He tried to keep his mind from straying back to it by thinking about Charlie. He imagined him curled up in a glass cage at the zoo, being offered plates of this, and bowls of that. People would press their noses against the glass and say: 'Oh, look at that beautiful little lizard! What pretty coloured scales!' They'd stand there staring for a while, hoping he'd do something, and when he didn't, they'd get bored and drift off to look for something more exciting. But he knew Charlie wasn't really in the zoo. Dad had just said that to cheer him up.

Twice, when he'd been half asleep, he'd thought Charlie had come back. He'd woken with a start, his heart thudding with joy. But the first time it had only been the branches of the apple tree scratching the window-pane; and the second time it had been Pudding that lay on his chest. Only the pulled-up threads of his bedspread, where Charlie had dragged them with his silver claws, remained as a reminder of his friend.

The sheet with the cut-out holes kept drifting back into his mind. He had asked Mum if she could try to make him a different costume this year. 'Just *try*,' he pleaded. But Mum said with Christmas coming she hadn't a moment, and anyway she'd found the snowman sheet in the linen cupboard and decided it would be just perfect for a ghost.

'You'll scare everyone out of their wits,' she added with satisfaction. It scared George out of his wits just to think about it, having to be steered round the hall again by Mrs Trimble.

How he wished Mum was like Mrs Throgmorton and 'clever with her needle'. He imagined the costumes she could make for him then: Long John Silver, complete with wooden leg and parrot (though the wooden leg might be a problem when he had to walk up to receive the prize); an Indian Chief with a plumage of magnificent feathers cascading down his back; a Viking with wings in his helmet. The costumes of his imagination seemed boundless in their ingenuity. But Mum could only 'cojjel'.

By his bed, still unopened, lay the bag of peanut brittle, the bubblegum, and the treacle toffee all stuck together now, in a solid, gooey lump. Oh, if only he'd been able to find what Charlie liked to eat he wouldn't have gone off like that. His puffs of smoke would have turned to magic flame, and the flame would have transformed him into something amazing. Now he would never see Charlie again, and his only hope had gone for good.

As the days went by the thunderclouds of worry over the Party hung heavily about his head. Five more days, four, three, two.

He couldn't concentrate at school either. He got all his sums wrong and for News, while the rest of the class were busy writing about all they'd done at home, the exciting costumes they were going to wear on Friday, and how busy their Mums and Dads were making them, George wrote:

'Got up. Went to school. Woched telly. Went to bed.'

Mrs Trimble asked George if anything was the matter. George sat there, shaking his head, saying nothing. There wasn't much you could say about last year's sheet. And how could he explain about Charlie? Who would believe him if he'd written that he'd found a real live dragon in the Fairy Grotto at Boddis

& Geerings and kept him for two whole days as a pet? And that now he was lost in Tarringtons' coal-yard, probably dead.

When Friday came he wondered whether he could pretend to be ill, but if he said he felt a bit sick Mum would say: 'Oh, it'll wear off, it's just excitement.' If he pretended to be really ill, groaning and rolling about in bed, clutching his stomach, she might get the doctor and that could be awkward.

George came home to dinner but he didn't feel like

eating. He pushed mince and mashed potato round his plate and wished it would go away.

'Eat up,' said Mum cheerfully. 'I've ironed your sheet. It's come up a treat. I shan't have time to meet you from school after the Party,' she added, squashing the sheet down into a plastic carrier bag. 'Mrs Toogood said she will see you home.'

'Mrs Bunting dear,' came the familiar voice from the landing, 'I've cut out another SUDZO voucher for you. You'll find it in the hall.'

Oh lucky Miss Prosser, thought George, with nothing to worry about and nothing to do all day but dust her pretty china ornaments and cut out SUDZO vouchers. No-one was going to cover her in an old sheet and send her to a party as a ghost.

Suddenly he felt he couldn't face the mince any more, or the sheet, or Miss Prosser and her SUDZO vouchers. He had half an hour before he need start back to school. He wandered round the side of the house and sat on the swing. It hung damp and limp from the leafless bough, and all the plants that in the summer had been so bright and colourful were shrivelled now and blackened by frost. It was only two o'clock but a grey and dreary afternoon and the house loomed out before him like a huge cardboard box with yellow squares of brightness where Mum and Miss Prosser upstairs had turned on the lights. He could see Mum in the bottom square, washing up at the sink, ramming plates into the rack. And in the top square he could see Miss Prosser sitting at her table with its lacy cloth, eating something dainty with a fork. People seemed different, George thought, when they didn't know you were watching them. Miss Prosser seemed lonely too.

Then something drew his eyes away from the yellow squares of light. From the coal bunker in the cellar something that looked like thin strands of smoke or steam were drifting lazily up the dark wall of the house, almost as though someone down there were boiling a kettle. And then . . . the little drifts became dense white puffs, too dense, too thick for any kettle. And slowly, as he watched, the white puffs turned slowly pink and a small blue flame appeared.

Chapter 14

'Charlie! Oh Charlie!'

George was speeding across the wet grass. He crouched by the coal chute and peered down into the cavernous depths of the cellar. Two red torches glowed from the blackness and made George blink.

'Charlie, what are you doing in the coal-hole? I've been thinking of you at Tarringtons all this time, lost and cold and hungry, and then I thought you must be dead.'

'No, I'm not dead,' said Charlie, his voice sounding very deep. 'I flew home last night and couldn't get in. This was the only hole I could squeeze into. I think I've had a bit too much to eat.'

'Too much of what?' called down George into the darkness, amazed that Charlie had been able to find anything to eat at all amongst all that coal, and even more amazed that it had obviously been something that had taken his fancy.

'Well, coal of course,' said Charlie, as though George were stupid to ask such an obvious question. 'Do you have any idea how many different sorts of coal you can eat?'

George had to admit that he'd never thought about it. He'd never really fancied a coal sandwich.

'Well, there's Anthracite and Coalite, Welsh Nuts and Stove Nuts, Phurnacite and . . .'

'And you've tried them all?' George interrupted, incredulous.

'I've tried everything that Tarringtons stocks, until I couldn't face another Stove Nut. I've crunched and I've scrunched, I've guzzled and gobbled, I've burrowed and tunnelled, I've whooshed and I've wriggled, I've slid and I've slithered, till my scales turned quite black, and nobody guessed I was there. Oh, those mountains of shining coal! That gleaming Anthracite! What a name! What magic!'

Magic! thought George. Now that Charlie had found what he really liked to eat and had filled himself up with it until he couldn't squeeze in another Stove Nut, perhaps now, at last . . .!

Crouching over the coal chute he told Charlie hurriedly about the Fancy Dress Party and the dreadful sheet that Mum expected him to wear for the second year running.

'You said you might be able to do magic,' reminded George, 'if we could find something you like to eat. And when you were puffing out your smoke just now, did you know it was turning pink? There was even a small blue flame!'

Charlie said he had noticed. After he'd licked all the coal-dust off he'd practised breathing fire, but there hadn't been anything to transform.

'Oh Charlie,' George begged, 'could you try, could you please try to cast a spell over the sheet and turn it into something?'

'What sort of something?' Charlie asked from the depths of the cellar. George still couldn't see him, only his ruby eyes which seemed now so very big.

'Oh, I don't know,' said George. 'Whatever comes into your mind. Anything would be more exciting than an old sheet with ripped-out holes and a felt pen smudge for a nose.'

'I don't think I could stay awake long enough,' said Charlie, his voice sounding even deeper and drowsier. 'All that gobbling and guzzling and scampering about has made me quite sleepy.'

'You can't go to *sleep*!' George exclaimed, horrified. 'Not now!' There was less than half an hour before the Party started. Why couldn't Charlie realise the urgency?

'George? Where are you, George?' Mum was calling from the kitchen window. 'It's gone half-past two!'

'Oh Charlie, you *must* help me! *Please*!'

Charlie said he'd try, if he didn't fall asleep first, but as he hadn't had any practice he couldn't be sure it would turn out right.

'I'll run and get the sheet,' said George quickly, before Charlie could change his mind.

'No, don't bother me now,' said Charlie, sounding sleepier than ever. 'Just take the sheet to school and wait for me there. What time does the Party start?'

'Three o'clock,' said George. 'I'll be waiting in the cloakroom.'

'GEORGE!' Mum was running out of patience.

'Three o'clock in the cloakroom,' Charlie slowly repeated.

'But how will you know where the cloakroom is?' asked George. 'You don't even know where the school is.'

'I'll find it,' said Charlie, 'if I'm still awake. Oh, and bring a ruler with you,' he added as an afterthought, 'and a saucer.'

'Whatever do you need a ruler and a saucer for?' asked George. But he got no reply. George had a dreadful sinking feeling that Charlie might already be asleep.

Chapter 15

In the cloakroom the rest of the class were already changing into their costumes. They were even more colourful and ingenious than last year: the Indian Chiefs of his imagination were there; so were the pirates and the Vikings, and Tom as a robot; and Fenella Throgmorton, of course, as Red Riding Hood, complete with her basket of eggs. George wanted to break the lot over her head and watch them dribble down the shiny red velvet.

He stood in the darkest, most inconspicuous corner of the cloakroom clutching the plastic carrier bag and wondering, with bated breath, about Charlie. How could a tiny dragon, no bigger than a lizard, possibly do anything to change that frayed old piece of sheet? He wouldn't even be able to find his way to school, let alone cast a spell. He would be curled up now, in the cellar, fast asleep. Wouldn't he?

But then he remembered something that Charlie had said about the way he had got home. He hadn't taken it in properly then – he had been so overjoyed at finding him again – but hadn't Charlie used the word 'fly'?

'What are you going as, George?' everyone asked.

'Surprise,' said George, clenching the carrier bag

more tightly so that no-one could look inside. The saucer and the ruler were wrapped up in the sheet, although he didn't know why he'd bothered to bring them.

'Well, aren't you going to put it on, whatever it is?' asked Fenella, looking down her nose at the crumpled plastic carrier bag. George could see a shiny leather case with FT in gold letters on the lid lying sedately on the seat under Fenella's peg.

'What have you got in there, anyway?' a boy dressed in purple satin knee-breeches and a gold cardboard crown asked, trying to snatch away the carrier bag, but George clenched it harder.

'I bet it's that awful old sheet again,' scoffed a Viking with wings on his helmet.

'You aren't allowed to go as the same thing two years running,' said Fenella smugly. 'Mrs Trimble said so.'

'I'm not,' said George, wishing a trapdoor would open in the floor so that he could fall through it.

Oh Charlie, please come, he willed.

Mrs Trimble appeared at the door, clapping her hands for silence.

'Come along, everybody,' she called out brightly. 'You should be in the hall by now. It's almost three o'clock.'

As everybody trooped out, chattering excitedly, George bent down to untie his shoelaces. Not that he needed to take his shoes off but at least it would look as if he had something to change into.

'Hurry up, George dear,' said Mrs Trimble kindly. 'You should have changed into your costume by now. Where is it?'

'In here,' said George, pointing to the carrier bag and wishing with all his heart that Mrs Trimble would go away. He was wondering whether the space beneath the bench was big enough to crawl into until the dreaded afternoon was over.

'Well, hurry up and get changed, then come to the hall as quickly as you can,' said Mrs Trimble, and to his relief she went.

George opened the door that led into the street.

Would anyone see if he just walked home? But Mum would wonder why he was back so soon. The street was bleak and cold and no-one was about. Everyone who didn't go to school would be sitting cosily by their fires, eating hot buttered toast, or shopping for Christmas presents in Boddis & Geerings. How lucky they all were! Some of them would be in the Fairy Grotto. He thought back to that Saturday afternoon when he'd first discovered Charlie and he had told George he was a dragon. Oh, if only that were true!

A church clock struck three.

Something was flying over the distant rooftops. It was too big for a bird. It must be an aeroplane, thought George, but it didn't seem quite the right shape, and there was no noise. No sun shone on that grey winter afternoon, but whatever it was sparkled like silver against the gloomy sky, then shone blue and yellow and pink as though lit by magic. And the wings weren't straight like those of an aeroplane, but arched and webbed and gleaming gold. As it swooped across the sky towards him, George could even see the outstretched claws of shining silver and the glowing eyes the colour of rubies.

The prickly feeling was back, running up George's spine, and his legs felt as floppy as Rosie's knitted doll with the stuffing leaking out. Could this amazing creature really be the tiny dragon who had lived in his pocket for two days and had curled up on his chest at night? Could it? Could this really be Charlie?

Chapter 16

As Charlie landed at the cloakroom door, he drew in his wings like two huge fans so that he could walk through it.

It was such a glorious moment that no words would possibly do. All such phrases like 'How you've grown!' were the sort of stupid remarks that aunts and uncles made when they came to stay. George wanted to say 'Now you're a proper dragon!' but that seemed stupid too.

But Charlie didn't seem to expect him to say anything.

'Now then, I've had my forty winks so let's get down to work,' he said briskly. He didn't seem lazy and sleepy any more, but full of energy. And he looked magnificent striding into the cloakroom, scales gleaming, the spines running down his back and tail like polished gold. George was almost disappointed that there was no-one left behind in the cloakroom to be amazed by his incredible friend.

'Well, where's the sheet?' he asked George.

George pulled out the sad piece of sheet from the carrier bag and laid it on the bench.

'And the ruler, and the saucer? You didn't forget those, I hope?'

'No, they're here too,' said George, diving his hand back into the bag, laying the ruler and the saucer on top of the sheet.

'Let's get a move on, then,' said Charlie, 'or the Party will be over and we shall miss all the fun.'

Fun? thought George. He had never thought of a Fancy Dress Party being fun.

'Don't just stand there,' said Charlie impatiently, sounding like Mum.

'What do you want me to do?' asked George. 'I thought it was you who had to work the spell.'

'I can't do it without your co-operation, can I?' said Charlie. 'Put the sheet on, of course.'

George struggled into it reluctantly. He had hoped Charlie would toss it away in disgust, but here he was actually having to put the thing on. The 'face' was at the back, and he had to grope around inside trying to find the holes.

A strange sound was coming from Charlie. Had he started the spell already? What would happen? Would he feel anything? Would he go hot? Or cold? Would his legs and arms go tingly? Would there be a sudden flash of lightning? Could he even be sure that Charlie would get the spell right?

He found the holes and tugged them round to match his eyes. But only one eye was able to peer out: Mum had got her measurements wrong and the other hole was somewhere between his left eye and his left ear.

It was only then that he realised that the strange

sound coming from Charlie wasn't the spell starting to work after all. It was Charlie laughing. He was rolling about the cloakroom, showing all his teeth in a vulgar way, holding his sides, and silver tears were running down his long snout. George was wondering anxiously if he would ever recover enough to be able to work the spell. He stood there, feeling foolish in the sheet, while Charlie collapsed in an exhausted heap on the bench.

'Now what?' asked George. 'Don't say you've forgotten what to do.'

'Of course I haven't forgotten,' said Charlie indignantly, having recovered himself at last. 'Hold the saucer in your left hand. No, not like that,' he said impatiently. 'Flat against your chest, with the bottom of the saucer facing outwards. Now hold the ruler in your right hand. That's it.'

George felt more ridiculous than ever. He was afraid Charlie would be overcome with mirth again, or that Mrs Trimble would come back to see why he was being so long.

'That's perfect,' said Charlie. 'Now hold it.' He sounded like the man who came once a year to take photos of the class, each of them posed singly in front of the blackboard, and each with a false smile and Mrs Trimble's vase of chrysanthemums stuck in the corner.

Charlie stepped back a few paces, then lowered his head so that his snout was in line with George's head. 'Now this may feel a bit warm,' he warned.

'You're not going to breathe fire over me?' George asked, horrified.

'How else do you expect the spell to work?' asked Charlie, impatient again. George really did ask the most idiotic questions.

'But I shall go up in flames,' said George, backing away.

'Keep still,' commanded Charlie. 'How do you expect me to concentrate when you keep moving around? Dragon flame isn't real fire. It doesn't burn, it just transforms.'

Charlie sounded so certain he knew what he was talking about that George stayed where he was, holding up the ruler in one hand, and the saucer pressed against his chest. He would just have to trust Charlie.

'Right,' said Charlie, 'here we go!' and he started to breathe out.

From Charlie's snout there came a deep and muffled sound, a rumbling, thundering sound. And then . . . shooting from his nostrils, like the sudden gush of water from a hose, two jets of flame of brightest blue, that melted slowly into purple, the purple into glowing red; blending through orange to a shimmering yellow: a glowing, golden rush of magic . . .

Chapter 17

George felt curiously warm, as though he were melting. And then he realised it wasn't he who was melting but the sheet. As Charlie breathed the golden fire on him the sheet was changing shape; it seemed to be folding in on him, encasing his arms and his legs, right down to his fingers and his toes; and he was aware of the whiteness of the sheet turning to silver. The hole through which his right eye had peered was now a long wide slit, and his head felt heavy as if he had a saucepan on his head. Oh, what had Charlie done? The saucer in his left hand had got heavier too, and it clanked against his chest.

It felt as though he had a tea-tray there. A saucepan and a tea-tray? What stupid idea had Charlie had? He lifted the ruler and that was heavy too. George squinted at it through his slit and almost dropped the flashing sword he found that he was holding. He stared amazed at his other hand that clasped a glinting shield! His arms seemed to be covered in something that looked like silver scales, or links, like chain mail, the sort of armour that knights wore when they fought dragons. Knights and dragons? Was it possible? Could it really be true that Charlie had transformed him into a knight in shining armour?

'Well, what else were you expecting to be?' asked Charlie. 'Little Miss Muffet? Come on, we're going to miss it all.'

'Are you coming too?' asked George. He hadn't ever imagined Charlie at the Party.

'Well you surely don't imagine I've come all this way just to sit and shiver in a gloomy cloakroom. And besides,' Charlie added, 'what good is a knight without a dragon?'

George tried to walk. Being a knight, he thought, was like trying to wade through treacle, covered from head to foot in dustbin lids which clanked at every step and rubbed your knees. But it made you so brave that you hardly noticed.

'Do you want to ride on my back?' suggested Charlie. 'That would make you look even braver.'

'How do I get up there? You're so huge now. Proper knights had to be dropped from hoists on to their horses.'

'Well there's no time to magic up a hoist,' said Charlie, and he lay as flat on the floor as he could manage, with his legs splayed out sideways. 'Watch that sword,' he warned as George scrambled over, 'I don't fancy that poking into my scales.'

George heaved himself between the golden spines. What with the shield and the sword he had no hands free to clasp round Charlie's neck, so he gripped his scaly back tightly with his knees.

'Right!' shouted Charlie, 'We're off!'

Clickety clack, clackety click! Four sets of silver

claws scuttling down the corridor sounded to George like hailstones hurled against the window-pane.

'FASTER! FASTER!' George yelled, as empty classrooms went whizzing past: blackboards, desks all flashing by.

Now they were at the door of the hall and charging through it as the party burst upon them.

George raised his shield and waved his flashing sword as Charlie let out a thunderous roar to announce their arrival.

And now he was aware of blazing lights and a sudden hush. Helmets, feathers, wings and wands, all blurred and merged together in a single whirling pool of colour: staring eyes and gaping mouths and hands that flew to frozen faces. Someone gasped and dropped his crown, another screamed and dropped her eggs. And then, like a film that stops and starts again, the hall came to life. Everyone, teachers and children, was herding across the floor in a sudden rush of panic, shouting and screaming to get out into the street.

'Well, that didn't last long,' said Charlie, disappointed. 'I told you we should miss the best part. Where are they all off to, do you suppose?' And before George could stop him, they were out in the street too, pursuing the terrified crowd through the town.

'STOP!' shouted George, 'Can't you see they think you're chasing them? Let's leave them and fly away.'

'Fly?' said Charlie, 'you wouldn't be able to hold on.'

'I would if I threw away my sword and shield,' said George, and he tossed them over a garden wall.

'Hold tight then,' said Charlie and, as George clasped him round the neck, his glowing golden wings unfolded.

Chapter 18

George threw back his visor and a rush of cold air swept past his face as the ground fell away beneath them and he was borne up and up, higher and higher, over the rooftops and over the trees. At last, thought George, this is what real dragons do in books! His heart was pounding but he felt amazingly brave. This was better than any space rocket. He was laughing and shouting, but he couldn't hear himself above the roar of golden fire shooting out from Charlie's nostrils.

The Fancy Dress Party, which had been streaming down the street like a swarm of scurrying ants, was now left far behind. Below them were houses no bigger than Lego, roads like rolls of tape unwinding, woolly blobs of trees in parks and, on that dull and dreary afternoon, lights appearing everywhere: street lights, strung out like rows of yellow beads, lights from houses clustered tightly, and lights so small they looked like the tops of little pins.

Charlie swooped and the houses and the roads, the trees and the lights swirled beneath them as though spun round on some huge revolving disc. Charlie's showing off, thought George, gripping his knees harder into Charlie's scales and clenching his arms still tighter round his neck. How he wished he could hold this most magical moment of all his life: he, George Bunting, whooshing and swooping through the air on a gleaming dragon! Hold it and stop it so that it would never fade away.

And now they were flying so high, up and up into the great silence of the sky, with the earth so far below, that they seemed to be suspended there, quite still. Charlie was no longer breathing his magic golden fire and all was quiet, so that for a moment it seemed as though his wish had come true and that time itself had stopped. Then up, still higher, through clouds like swirling steam, and into a burst of light: a sky of brightest blue that melted into palest yellow, and turned to deepest pink where a huge and glowing ball of red was turning the clouds below into great puffs of rose and gold that stretched away beneath them to the very edge of the sky.

All at once George realised he was no longer a knight. Charlie's magic must have worn off because he was back in the old sheet, with the strip of elastic that Mum had 'cojjelled' round the neck to keep it on. But now it didn't matter because all he wanted to do was to leap off Charlie's back and tumble about in the clouds, bouncing and burrowing, as on an everlasting bed of pillows.

'Can you breathe on the clouds, Charlie, to make them solid so we don't fall through?'

So Charlie did and turned them into something that wasn't quite like pillows, or candyfloss, or snow,

but a mixture of all three. And they leaped and
danced and rolled and turned cartwheels until they
were quite puffed out.

'It's nearly dark,' said George. 'It must be time for
tea.'

'Climb on my back, then,' said Charlie, 'before the
magic fades and we tumble through.'

What if it doesn't fade, and we have to stay up here
for ever? wondered George, feeling suddenly not
brave any more. But no sooner had he scrambled on

to Charlie's back than the cloud into which Charlie was sinking his silver claws dissolved, drifting and separating in wispy strands to form a hole through which they plunged so fast that George's ears were popping. He could see through one frayed hole the town swirling up to meet them with amazing speed.

They landed on a hill and sat staring at the blobs of light below them, a dragon and a ghost in a torn-up sheet.

'I don't think anyone enjoyed the Fancy Dress Party this year,' said Charlie sadly. 'Why did they all rush out like that when we arrived? It wasn't very sociable.'

'I expect that's the last one they'll ever have,' said George, relieved. 'Thanks for the magic,' he added. It sounded stupid, as though he were thanking Miss Prosser for a piece of cherry cake, but no sort of thank-you would seem right for being changed into a knight and riding on a dragon and turning cart-wheels on a cloud.

'Well,' said Charlie suddenly, 'I must be off.'

'Off?' repeated George. 'Off where?'

'Oh, I don't know,' said Charlie, 'just off.'

'You don't stay anywhere long, do you?' George said, suddenly sad. 'Why don't you come home first and have some tea?'

'You've forgotten, I loathe scrambled egg,' Charlie reminded him.

'Well, you could stop off at Tarringtons for a sack or two of Anthracite,' suggested George. 'Dad would pay,' he added, realising for the first time that someone should have paid Tarringtons for Charlie's fortnight's feasting.

He was trying to make the magic last just a bit longer, although he knew the time had come to say goodbye to Charlie – the dragon was too big to sleep on his bed now, and how would he explain to Miss Prosser, hovering on the landing in her silky mauve dress, that Charlie was just another friend he'd brought home to tea?

'I told you, I couldn't face another Stove Nut,' Charlie said. 'I'm stocked up now for the winter.'

'Will you come back?' asked George.

'Some day, perhaps; after I've fought a proper knight on a white horse, and gobbled up a few Princesses on the way.'

'Can you take me home before you fly away to do that?' asked George.

His arms felt numb and stiff as they clasped Charlie's neck for the last time and they swooped down from the hill. They were now so low they could hear an old man muttering as he stooped to pick up the rubbish tossed over his garden wall: 'Sweet wrappers, crisp packets, bits of fish-and-chip paper, and now a ruler and a saucer. Where will it all end?' he grumbled to himself.

'Just one thing before I go,' said Charlie as he left George at his gate. 'Don't throw away the sheet. It may come in handy one day,' he added mysteriously.

And then, before George could turn round, Charlie

was just a gleaming blob disappearing over the rooftops.

He didn't say goodbye, thought the ghost in the sheet as it groped its way up the path.

'Oh, there you are,' said Mum, stirring custard on the stove. 'Oh George, fancy coming home like that. Couldn't you bear to take it off?'

George went over to the window and looked out through the frayed hole at the sky, now quite dark and sprinkled with stars. Mum was beating the wooden spoon about in the saucepan, trying to get the lumps of custard out, but he couldn't hear her. He was staring at a stream of yellow stars that, as he watched, were not like stars at all. The stream was like a long unwinding roll of fire. And as he watched, the stream formed loops, and the loops became letters. He started to read the letters as they unfolded: a 'g', an 'o' and then another 'o', a 'd', a 'b', a 'y' and then an 'e'. The yellow stars streamed on until, twisting and curling and looping again, they formed a 'g', and an 'e', an 'o' and an 'r', another 'g' and an 'e'. Then, like a thread of yellow wool that breaks in strands, they came to an end. Charlie stared at the letters spread out across the sky for all the world to read, until one by one they seemed to melt like snow before the sun: first the 'g' and then the 'o', another 'o' and then the 'd', until only one 'e', right at the very end, was left. And then that too dissolved, and the stream of yellow stars was gone, as though it had never been.

'Well,' said Mum, holding up the wooden spoon, so that the custard trickled down the side of the pan, 'tell me how the Party went. Did you scare them out of their wits?'

'Yes,' said George, 'I scared them out of their wits and out of the school. They all ran screaming up the street.'

'There,' said Mum with a satisfied smile, 'what did I tell you? The simplest costumes are the best.'

'And I danced with a dragon,' went on George, 'and turned cartwheels on a cloud. And I saw the sun turn the clouds into puffs of pink and gleaming gold.'

'Did you, my love?' said Mum. 'Well, that was nice.' And, banging the edge of the bowl with the wooden spoon, she dolloped out the custard.